# A PIECE OF CAKE

by LeUyen Pham

SCHOLASTIC INC.

**It** was Little Bird's birthday.
Mouse, who was a very kind
mouse, made her a cake.

He worked the whole morning
through and used up everything
in his pantry.

Mouse began to walk to Little Bird's home.
On the way, he met Chicken, sitting with all her eggs.

Hello, Chicken!

said Mouse.

Chicken said,

Mouse didn't think Little Bird would need a cork.

But Mouse was a very kind mouse.

Surely Little Bird would
not mind if I gave
Chicken some of her cake.

So Mouse traded one piece of cake
for the cork and went on his way.

Next, Mouse met Squirrel, who was gathering nuts.

Hello, Squirrel!

said Mouse.

Squirrel said,

Gadzooks, that's one tasty-looking cake! Mouse, old buddy, how about giving me some? If you give me a piece of cake, I'll trade you . . .

NUTS for NUTS

Mouse couldn't imagine that Little Bird would need a wire.

But Mouse was a very kind mouse.

Surely Little Bird would
not mind if I gave
Squirrel some of her cake.

So Mouse traded one piece of cake
for the wire and went on his way.

Soon, Mouse met Bear, surrounded by his many pots of honey.

Hello, Bear!

said Mouse.

Bear said,

Wowsers, that's one tasty-looking cake! Mouse, my fine little fellow, would you mind giving me some? If you give me a piece of cake, I'll trade you . . .

Mouse was *sure* that Little Bird did not want a net.

But Mouse was a very kind mouse.

Surely Little Bird would not mind if I gave Bear some of her cake.

So Mouse traded one piece of cake for the net and went on his way.

Farther on, Mouse met Cow, who
was surrounded by bottles of milk.

said Mouse.

Cow said,

Holy cow, that cake looks good! Mouse, my dear, may I have some? If you give me a piece of cake, I'll trade you . . .

Mouse knew that Little Bird would *not* want a flyswatter.

But Mouse was a very kind mouse.

Surely Little Bird would
not mind if I gave
Cow some of her cake.

So Mouse traded the last
piece of cake for the flyswatter
and went on his way.

Finally, he reached Little Bird's house.

Oh, Little Bird! I wanted to bring you a cake for your birthday. But I traded the pieces of cake for a cork, a wire, a net, and a flyswatter. I would make you another cake, but I've used up everything in my pantry.

I'm so sorry.

But Little Bird, who was
a very clever bird, said,

Oh, but Mouse! These are
wonderful presents! Come
with me and I'm sure
we'll find a use for them.

First, they met Cow.

And Little Bird twisted the wire into a loop, dipped it into the soap, and blew bubbles.

**WOW!** said Cow.

So Cow traded the milk for the wire, and Mouse and Little Bird went on their way.

Next, they met Bear.

What's wrong, Bear?

asked Mouse.

And Little Bird popped the cork into the hive to keep the bees from coming out.

**Excellent!**

said Bear.

So Bear traded the honey for the cork, and Mouse and Little Bird went on their way.

**Well,**

said clever Little Bird,

**Squirrel, my friend, if
you give us some nuts,
we'll give you . . .**

And Little Bird bent the flyswatter in the ground, loaded it with nuts, and let it go. The nuts flew through the air and landed in the nest.

Cool!

said Squirrel.

So Squirrel traded some nuts for the flyswatter, and Mouse and Little Bird went on their way.

Finally, they met Chicken.

**Yay!** said Chicken.

So Chicken traded two eggs for the invitation and ran off to tell the others.

And Mouse and Little Bird went on to Mouse's home.

Mouse and Little Bird worked all that afternoon, and together they made a cake that looked and tasted even better than the first one.

After everyone was given a piece, Mouse gave Little Bird one last present.

ISBN 978-0-545-94073-3

Copyright © 2014 by LeUyen Pham. All rights reserved.
Published by Scholastic Inc.,
557 Broadway, New York, NY 10012,
by arrangement with Balzer + Bray, an imprint of
HarperCollins Children's Books,
a division of HarperCollins Publishers.
SCHOLASTIC and associated logos are trademarks
and/or registered trademarks of Scholastic Inc.

12 11 10 9 8 7 6 5 4 3 2 1          16 17 18 19 20 21

Printed in the U.S.A.                              40

This edition first printing, January 2016

The illustrations for this book were rendered
in pencil and colored digitally.
Typography by Dana Fritts and LeUyen Pham

For Mike and Chris,
who helped me make the cake,
and for Adrien,
who gets to eat it